THUD & BLUNDER

Raintree is an imprint of Capstone Global Library Limited, a company
incorporated in England and Wales having its registered office at 264 Banbury
Road, Oxford, OX2 7DY – Registered company number: 6695582

www.raintree.co.uk
myorders@raintree.co.uk

Edited by Julie Gassman
Designed by Steve Mead
Original illustrations © Capstone Global Library Limited 2017
Illustrated by Pol Cunyat
Production by Steve Walker
Originated by Capstone Global Library Limited
Printed and bound in China

ISBN 978 1 4747 2458 6
20 19 18 17 16
10 9 8 7 6 5 4 3 2 1

British Library Cataloguing in Publication Data
A full catalogue record for this book is available from the British Library.

THUD & BLUNDER

THE
NOT-SO-DEADLY
DRAGON

Written by
SEAN TULIEN

Illustrated by
POL CUNYAT

raintree
a Capstone company — publishers for children

Thud is the daughter of the town's blacksmith. She's skilled with a hammer, whether she's pounding out dings in Blunder's armour or thumping a monster. Thud is equal parts brains and brawn!

THE TOWER & FOREST

What **Blunder** lacks in size and smarts, he makes up for in foolishness. He fearlessly charges into danger, whether it's real or not. He wields his mighty broad sword and never backs down from a monster.

CHAPTER 1

FIGHTING FIRE WITH SWORDS

"FIRE! FIRE!" cried the villagers.

Every building on the northern side of Village Town was in flames!

Some of the villagers threw water on the burning buildings. Some simply threw up. But all of them panicked.

Thankfully, two nine-year-old knights, Thud and Blunder, had heard their cries. In moments, the two heroes were throwing buckets of water onto the burning buildings.

Soon the adventurers had put out all the fires. But despite their brave efforts, several buildings had burnt to the ground.

Thud wiped sweat from her forehead. "How did this happen?" she asked.

"How did this happen, you ask?" An old man limped over to them. "Why, those fires were started by the breath of a great red dragon."

Blunder's eyes twinkled. "A **DRAGON**?!" he cried. "I've always wanted to slay a dragon!"

"Just wait. How can you be sure a dragon is to blame?" Thud asked the old man.

"I'm old. Old people know things," the man explained. "The beast dwells in a cave at the top of Mount Mountain, just north of Village Town."

"Let's go!" Blunder shouted.

Thud held her friend back. "Before we talk about slaying anything," she said, "let's make sure this dragon is evil – and **GUILTY** – first."

The man leaned forward. "And he's very evil," the man said. "I've heard countless tales of his evil deeds."

Thud narrowed her eyes. "Go on."

The man held up a finger. "He breathes fire!" the man said. He held up a second finger. "He steals treasure!" he said. He held up a third finger. "And, most evil of all, he makes **BABIES CRY!**"

Blunder gasped. "Crying babies?!"

"Yes," the old man said. "And if someone doesn't stop him, the entire town will be *filled* with crying babies." And with that, the man hobbled away.

After the man was out of sight, Blunder grabbed Thud by the shoulders. "We need to get up that mountain and stop that dragon," he said. "And fast!"

Thud rubbed her chin. "Agreed," she said. "I'll call Elliot."

Thud pressed two fingers to her mouth. She let loose the loudest whistle of all time. **TWEET!**

Soon, they heard a **CLOPPITY-CLOP-CLOP!** Within seconds, a hornless unicorn appeared.

"Hey, Elliot!" Thud said. "Ready for a ride?"

Elliot rose up on his rear legs in glee. **"NEIGH!"** he said, pawing the air with his hooves.

"Are you sure?" Thud said. "Because we're going on an **ADVENTURE!**"

Elliot whinnied with joy. He snorted, then trotted over to them and lowered his head.

Blunder lifted his leg and jumped onto Elliot. But instead of landing in the saddle, Blunder fell off the other side and landed on his face with a **THUD!**

"NEIGH-HEHE," Elliot neighed.

With a smirk on her face, Thud leaped up and took Elliot's reins.

Blunder scrambled onto the hornless unicorn's back behind her. "Are you okay?" Thud asked. "You fell pretty hard."

Blunder linked his arms around her waist. "Elliot moved," he grumbled.

Thud giggled. "Onward, Elliot!" she said. "To the tippy-top of Mount Mountain!"

CHAPTER 2

AN UNCOMMON COLD

With the sun hanging high in the sky, Elliot galloped up the mountain carrying Thud and Blunder. The hornless unicorn was as fast as fast can be. Unfortunately, Elliot got bored easily. Along the way, the not-so-trusty steed stopped several times to sniff woodland creatures, eat pretty flowers and trot in circles.

But eventually the three made it to the top of Mount Mountain. Elliot came to a stop outside the mouth of a dark cave.

"NEIGH!" the hornless unicorn neighed at the cavern.

Thud patted Elliot's side. "It's okay, buddy. It's just a bit dark."

"NEIGH!" Elliot neighed. He shook them both off his back. They tumbled to the ground. **THUD-WHUMP!** Elliot turned and galloped back down the mountain, neighing all the way.

"What is his problem?" Blunder said, rubbing his head.

Thud dusted herself off. "Maybe he's afraid of the dark," she said, pointing at the cave.

Blunder stood. He eyed the cave. "It's pretty dark in there," he said, not at all scared of the dark (not one bit).

Thud smirked. "I'll go first," she said. "If you want."

Blunder stuck out his upper lip. "No, Thud," he said. "I shall take the lead." He turned on his heel and marched toward the cave.

AH-CHOOOOM! Fire roared out from the cave!

Blunder dodged just in time, narrowly avoiding the flames. The two adventurers watched the fire tumble down the mountainside.

"Well," Blunder said, getting to his feet. "At least we know we're in the right place."

Thud pointed. **"FIRE!"** she cried.

"Duh," Blunder said. "It almost burnt me to a crisp!"

Thud pointed at Blunder. **"FIRE!"** she repeated.

Blunder sniffed the air. "Is something burning?" he asked.

Thud pointed at Blunder's head. **"YOUR. HAIR. IS. ON. FIRE!"**

Blunder's eyes went wide. **"AHHH!"** he cried. He ran in circles, bravely flailing his hands over his head.

Thud ran at Blunder and tackled him to the ground. **SLAP! SLAP! SLAP!**

She patted his head over and over until
the flames died out.

They lay on the ground, panting.
"That's two fires we've put out today,"
Thud said. She sat up and leaned over
Blunder. "Are you hurt?"

"Pain is stupid!" Blunder said, raising his weapon. **"TO BATTLE!"** He jumped up and dashed into the cave.

Thud grabbed her hammer. "Wait!" she said, running after him. "You don't know what's –"

Thud skidded to a halt. The biggest dragon she'd ever seen stood in the rear of the cave. His red scales glittered in the orange-red light blooming from the torches hanging on the walls.

The great red beast sat atop a huge pile of gold, weapons and other treasures. And there, at the dragon's feet, Blunder let loose a flurry of blows against the dragon's leg!

THWACK! SMACK! SCHWING!

"I'm just getting warmed up!" Blunder cried.

The dragon stared wide-eyed down
at Blunder. Even though the blows did
no harm to his thick, scaly skin, the
fearsome beast burst into tears!

Blunder stopped his attack. "Is the
dragon . . . crying?" he asked.

The beast whimpered. He hunched down to the ground and pulled his pile of treasure closer to his belly.

"Why did you hit me?" the dragon cried.

Blunder raised his weapon. "You set my hair on fire!" he cried.

"I didn't mean to," the dragon whined. "I'm sick. I have a very bad hot."

Blunder lowered his weapon – just a little. "A 'hot'?" he asked.

Thud carefully stepped over a strange, charred hole in the ground as she approached them. "I think he means he has a cold," she said to Blunder. "Only, you know, he breathes fire."

The dragon smiled a little and nodded. "I sneeze fire!" he said, oddly proud of the fact.

SNIFFLE! SNIFFLE! Snotty magma dripped from his nostrils and melted some of the treasure below.

"YIKES!" Blunder said, leaping back. He narrowed his eyes at the dragon. "Are you evil?"

The dragon sighed. "No," he said. "Why does everyone think that?"

Blunder dropped his weapon. "Aww, man. I really wanted to slay a dragon."

Thud rolled her eyes. "So what's your name?" she asked.

The dragon smiled shyly. "My name is Thermatrixxitalicus," he said.

Blunder looked up in awe. *"The* Thermatrixxitalicus?" he cried. "The great and terrible red dragon of fiery death and destruction?!"

Thermatrixxitalicus sniffled. "My friends call me Thermy," he mumbled.

Thud smiled up at the not-so-deadly dragon. "Good to meet you, Thermy. I'm Thud." She gestured at her friend. "And this is Blunder."

Blunder bowed. "'Tis a pleasure to meet you," he said.

Thermy's wings wiggled excitedly. "Ooh, you're fancy!" he said, clapping his tiny hands together.

Blunder poked Thud. "I like this monster," he whispered.

Thermy snorted and sniffled. **AH-CHOOOM!** Flames blazed out of his mouth and nose, barely missing Thud and Blunder's heads.

Blunder felt his hair to make sure he wasn't a walking matchstick – again.

"We've really got to something about his sneezing," he said.

"Yeah . . ." Thud said. "No offence, Thermy, but you're kind of burning down Village Town."

Thermy frowned. "I'm so very sorry about that," the dragon said. "I don't want to hurt anyone. I just can't stop sneezing."

Thud pulled out a handkerchief and handed it to Thermy. "Here. This should do the trick."

Thermy shook his head and sighed. "I'm afraid that won't do. The only thing that can stop my sneezes is the Holy Handkerchief, and someone stole it."

"Do you know who took it?" Thud asked.

"A Lava Giant," Thermy grumbled. He pointed at the charred hole in the ground. "She lives with her baby under the mountain. She dug her way up, snuck in while I slept and stole my handkerchief."

Blunder's eyes went wild with burning justice. "I, Blunder, vow to return the Holy Handkerchief to you!" he vowed.

Thermy's little wings wiggled with joy. "You will help me?" he asked.

Thud patted the dragon's knee. "Sure!" she said. "It seems like that would solve everybody's problems."

Thermy clapped his tiny hands together. "Great!" he said. He paused, then added, "But be careful. It's a long way – **AH-CHOOM!**" Thermy sneezed hot fire over their heads yet again. He sniffled. "It's a long way down."

"TO BATTLE!" Blunder said. He leaped into the tube.

Thermy smirked. "My, he's very brave!" he said to Thud.

Thud sighed. "I better catch up with him," she said.

"Be safe!" Thermy said. He smiled and waved his tiny hand at her.

Thud nodded. Then she slid into the chute.

CHAPTER 3

LIKE STEALING CANDY

"WHEEEE!" Blunder squealed.

"This is awesome!" Thud cried.

The two brave adventurers flew down the chute. Even though they were sure to soon face their doom, it was the most fun they'd had in days.

PLOP! PLOP! They landed in a huge cavern. They were just a few feet away from a huge, bubbling pool of lava.

Hot, oozing magma bled from cracks in nearby walls. Little streams of lava ran like veins through the rocky ground.

Blunder began to fan his face, which had began to drip. "Is it hot in here," he said, "or is it just me?"

Thud wiped her brow and glanced around. "I think Mount Mountain might actually be a volcano," she said.

Blunder gulped. "Do you think it's . . . active?"

Thud shrugged. "Let's just find this Holy Handkerchief as fast as we can."

The two walked toward the other side of the cave. They stepped around and over thin rivers of lava until they reached a jagged group of rocks.

"It looks like a pointy bed," Blunder said, looking at the rocks.

In the centre of the rocks was a watermelon-sized boulder. Stuck between the boulder and the rocks was a white piece of cloth.

"There it is!" Blunder said. He reached out, grabbed a corner of the cloth and pulled.

The handkerchief didn't budge. "What gives?" Blunder said. He pulled harder, grunting with effort.

RUMBLE. The boulder rolled to its side. Little rocky arms and legs appeared. Three little holes appeared in what looked like a head. The thing turned its childlike face toward Blunder. Then it burst into lava-tears!

"WAH! WAH!"

"What is that thing?!" Blunder cried. "And where's the Lava Giant?"

"If I had to guess, I'd say it's the Lava Giant's baby," Thud said. She glanced left and right. The Lava Giant was surely somewhere nearby.

Blunder reached out and pulled the square of fabric again. **FLOOP!** With one heroic tug, he freed the Holy Handkerchief!

Blunder held the magical item above his head. **"VICTORY!"** he cried, dancing in celebration.

The Lava Giant Baby glanced up at Blunder. Its eyes grew wider and wider.

It cried even harder. **"WAHHHHH!"**

Blunder stopped dancing. "Did I just steal a baby's blankie?" he mumbled.

"BABY!" came a rocky growl. **"BABY OKAY?"**

Blunder froze. "Uh-oh," he said. "I think I stole the wrong baby's blanket."

WHUMP. WHUMP. WHUMP.

Footfalls echoed through the stone halls. Thud and Blunder turned around. A giant twice as big as Thermy stood before them.

The Lava Giant bent down to face the knights and flexed her rocky muscles.

"YOU GIVE BLANKIE BACK TO BABY!" she bellowed. **"YOU GIVE BLANKIE BACK TO BABY RIGHT NOW!"**

Thud and Blunder gulped.

They looked at each other.

They looked at the Lava Giant.

Then they bravely ran away.

CHAPTER 4

FIRE SAFETY

The two heroes ran until they returned to the lava chute. The opening to the chute was much too high for them to reach themselves, and they didn't think the giant would help them.

They were trapped.

WHUMP. WHUMP. WHUMP. The Lava Giant came to a stop just in front of them. She raised her rocky fist into the air and growled.

Blunder's shoulders sank. "We're doomed."

But Thud refused to give up. "Not yet!" she said. She grabbed Blunder's arm.

They ran alongside the edge of the lava pool. **"COME AND GET IT!"** Thud yelled.

The Lava Giant pounded her chest and chased them.

Thud and Blunder continued to run along the edge of the lava. As the giant bounded after them, her feet caught the edge of the pool and the stone crumbled. The great monster fell into the lava with a loud **SPLOOSH!**

Thud and Blunder stopped running. Thud pumped her fist in the air and yelled, **"YES!"**

Then the lava began to churn and bubble. **RRRRUMBLE!** A great rumbling shook the cavern.

"What's happening?" Blunder yelled over the noise.

Thud grinned. "The volcano is about to explode!"

Blunder looked like he'd seen a ghost. "Why aren't you worried?"

Thud yanked the hankie from Blunder's grip and tossed it onto the lava's surface. Sure enough, it didn't melt. Then Thud jumped onto the floating hankie. "Get on!" she yelled.

Blunder screamed as he leaped. He landed safely next to Thud.

FWOOOOM! The surge of lava carried them up, up, up – into the lava chute! Thud clenched her teeth and held tight. Blunder screamed bravely as the lava pushed them up the chute.

They reached a split in the chute. Thud cried, "Lean to the left!"

WOOSH! The Holy Handkerchief shifted left. They went flying into the side-chute . . .

. . . and landed on the stone floor of Thermy's cave!

Blunder's breaths were fast and shallow. "That . . . that was . . ."

Thud helped him to his feet. "Scary, yeah," she said. "But we made –"

"THAT WAS AWESOME!" Blunder cried. "Let's do it again!"

Thermy waddled over to them. "You're back!" he said.

Thud bent over and picked up the Holy Handkerchief. "We are," Thud said. "And we brought your handkerchief back." She handed it to Thermy.

Happy, sizzling tears ran down the dragon's cheeks. "You truly are great adventurers," he sniffled.

Blunder wrapped his arm around Thud. "It was our pleasure," Thud said. Blunder nodded.

Thermy said, "How can I ever tha-thank –"

Blunder covered his head.

AH-CHOOOOOM!

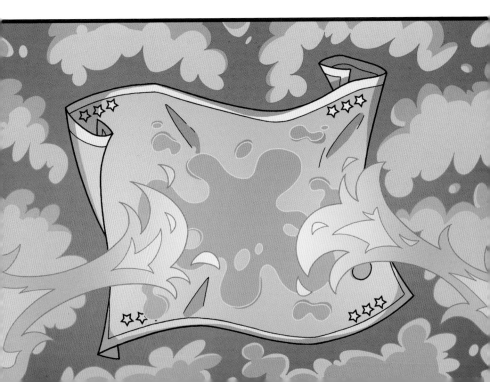

The Holy Handkerchief was covered in dragon snot, but it had stopped the flames!

"It worked!" Thud cried.

Thermy nodded. "How can I ever repay you?" he finished.

Blunder pointed at the gold nuggets beneath Thermy's feet. "Can we have some of your treasure?" he asked.

Thermy tilted his head. "You want that?" he asked. "Why?"

Blunder rolled his eyes. "Duh – to buy stuff!" he said.

Thud elbowed him. "Maybe you should ask nicely," she said with a smile.

Blunder dropped his sword. He bent to one knee and held one hand to his chest. He placed his other hand out to the side with an open palm.

"O, mighty and sneeze-y dragon," he said. "Wouldst thou be so kind to give me a few pieces of thine gold nuggets?"

Thermy wiggled his wings. "Such a gentleman!" he said. "How could I say no?"

Blunder did a little dance.

Thermy scratched his head with a claw. "These nuggets are old, though," he said. "Do you want newer ones?"

Blunder shrugged. "Why not!" he said.

Thermy waddled over to a corner of the cave. "Coming right up," he said over his shoulder. He squatted low to the ground and closed his eyes. His whole body tightened.

Thud raised an eyebrow. "Thermy . . . what are you doing?"

"Making new ones," Thermy said.

"What?" was all Blunder said.

PLOOP! A golden nugget fell from the dragon's rear. The beast picked it up, waddled over to Blunder, and held it out to him. "Here you go," Thermy said.

Thud started laughing.

Blunder looked at the nugget. He looked at Thermy. "That came from your bottom," he said.

Thermy dropped the nugget at Blunder's feet. "Well, yeah," he said. "Where else would it come from?"

Blunder scratched his head. "I . . . don't know," he said. "I figured you'd just been collecting them for years."

"Years?" he said. "These are just from the last few days of being sick. It hurt to move, so I didn't get up to go to the toilet."

Thud laughed even harder.

Blunder bent over and picked up the gold nugget. "Treasure is treasure," he said, shoving it into his pocket.

While Blunder pocketed more nuggets, Thermy stretched his neck out toward Thud. "Your friend is weird," he whispered.

Thud smirked. "Tell me about it."

"NEIGHHHHH!" Just then, Elliot burst through the cave's mouth. As he pawed the air with his hooves, Thud saw he was wearing magical Unicorn Battle Armour!

"Nice armour, Elliot!" Blunder cooed.

Thud walked over and patted the hornless unicorn's flank. "Is that why you left earlier?" Thud asked. "To get ready for battle?"

Elliot nodded proudly. He pawed the ground with a hoof, ready to charge Thermy.

"Whoa, there," Thud said, holding him back. "Thermy's a friend!"

Elliot snorted out a sigh. He cantered outside and turned around, waiting for them to follow.

"I guess our ride's here," Thud said to Thermy.

Thermy smiled from wing to wing. "Thanks again," he said. He waved his Holy Hanky at them. "Safe travels!"

Just then, Thud spotted something in Thermy's pile of treasure. She walked over and picked up what looked like a spikey weapon. She rubbed her chin. "Hey, Thermy," she said. "Can I have this?"

Thermy wiggled his wings. "Sure," he said. He pointed at Thud's hammer. "But why? You already have a weapon."

"It's not for me," Thud said. "And it's only a weapon if you use it like one."

"Good point," Thermy said. "Who is it for then?"

Thud walked over the hole in the cave, held the spikey object over it, and then let go. She leaned down and cupped her hand to her ear. She listened to it tumble **DOWN, DOWN, DOWN,** until . . .

Talk About the Tale!

1. The people of Village Town all thought Thermy was evil. How do you think that made Thermy feel?

2. Thermy had piles of gold nuggets in his cave. Why do you think he never shared them with the people of Village Town?

3. What did the old man tell Thud and Blunder to make them think the dragon was evil? Should they have believed him?

Write About the Adventure!

1. Blunder marched into the cave without thinking and got hit by Thermy's fiery sneeze. Have you ever done something without thinking first? Write about it.

2. Think about the Holy Handkerchief. Make a list of words or phrases that describe the handkerchief. Try to list at least five things.

3. Thud gave the Lava Baby a rattle, but it still didn't have its blankie. Do you think the Lava Giant went back to Thermy's cave to try and steal the Holy Handkerchief again? Write a story where she does just that.

GLOSSARY

adventurer anyone who looks for adventure and danger and Evil, with a capital *E*

canter to run kind of fast, between a trot and a gallop

destruction what happens when a great and terrible red dragon burns things with its fiery breath

fearsome frightening or scary, like a great and terrible red dragon with fiery breath

gallop to run so fast that all your legs leave the ground at once – wee!

handkerchief also called a hankie, for short; a square piece of cloth used for wiping boogies from your nose

slay to kill, which is what adventurers try to do to a great and terrible red dragon with fiery breath

smirk to smile in a knowing, silly or annoying way

steed an animal that someone rides, most often a horse or camel, but possibly a hornless unicorn if you are an adventurer

whimper to make quiet, crying noises; not something you'd expect a great and terrible red dragon with fiery breath to do

ABOUT THE CREATORS

ABOUT the AUTHOR

Author Sean Tulien works as a children's book editor in Seatle, Washington, USA. In his free time, Sean likes to read, eat sushi, exercise outdoors, listen to loud music, play with his quirky bunny, Habibi, and his curious hamster, Buddy, and spend time with his brilliant wife, Nicolle. When he's not doing all that stuff, Sean loves to write books like this one.

ABOUT the ILLUSTRATOR

 Illustrator Pol Cunyat was born in 1979 in Sant Celoni, a small village near Barcelona, Spain. As a child, Pol always dreamed of being an illustrator. So he went to study illustration in Escola De Còmic Joso de Barcelona and Escola D'Art, Serra i Abella de L'Hospitalet. Now, Pol makes a living doing illustration work for various publishers and studios. Pol's dream has come true, but he will never stop dreaming.

Check out more
THUD & BLUNDER
Adventures!

THE NOT-SO-DEADLY DRAGON

by SEAN TULIEN

THE NOT-SO-HEROIC KNIGHT

by BLAKE HOENA

THE NOT-SO-HELPLESS PRINCESS

by BLAKE HOENA

THE NOT-SO-EVIL WIZARD

by SEAN TULIEN

For MORE GREAT BOOKS go to
WWW.RAINTREE.CO.UK